Allied Invasion of Sicily
A World War II Novel

Richard G. Hole

World War II

SYNOPSIS

The always unpleasant fog prevented complete visibility. The British aircraft were flying in perfect formation in the direction of the predetermined objective. In the center of it the bombing devices were placed and covering these the fighters flew. Barely a quarter of an hour had passed since they had left the Africa base and were heading for the islands where they were to drop their deadly charges...

Allied Invasion of Sicily is a story belonging to the World War II collection, a series of war novels set in World War II.

ALLIED INVASION OF SICILY

CHAPTER I

DEFINE A NEED

"That's right, gentlemen, my words strictly adhere to reality. It is necessary, completely necessary to proceed to the occupation of the three islands of the Sicilian channel, because they are in fact the bridge that will take us to the Sicilian objective. It would be completely impossible to jump on the island, leaving Pantelleria, Lampedusa and Linosa aside .

Those who were there listening to Eisenhower's wise words made an affirmative gesture from time to time, as if expressing their agreement with the general's words. He kept talking.

"These three small islands, which are not territorially important, are actually of great strategic value to us. I don't think it's easy to get hold of them. The Italians will have them well defended, which is why I think it is extremely dangerous to overturn our landing troops without having previously intensely bombarded the areas of operation. Of this, as is logical, the aviation will be in charge with the support of the navy. Any questions?

An aviation colonel, who had several decorations on his chest, tall, thin and with a somewhat childish face, asked:

"When should these bombings start?

Eisenhower, smiling, replied to the questioner:

"The order is already given.

"Which means...?

"That they should start immediately.

There was a few moments of silence during which the breathing of those assembled could be heard.

It was the first days of April. The days were hot, and they continually lengthened. The sun, second by second, was beating the darkness of the night. But it had already fallen completely when even inside the house the movement of those gathered in it could be seen. The meeting lasted for several hours, which came to show the importance of the issues that were discussed and developed during the course of the meeting.

Eisenhower, pointing with a long pointer, parts of a large map that was hanging on one of the walls. The map represented the northeastern part of Africa, Sicily and southern Italy.

"... that's the plan of operations" finished the general, turning to look at those gathered.

One of them, getting up, asked:

"Does the general think the Italians will put up a lot of resistance to our landing?

The smiling general answered the question in the following terms:

"It is natural that they oppose, but if it will be a lot or a little, I cannot answer that, until we are on the march.

"Understand.

"The islands themselves," Eisenhower began again, "are poor, so if we close off the supply groups, they won't be able to withstand our continued siege for long. And once our forces are stationed on those little islands, the rest is as easy as possible.

The general's words seemed to please those gathered, who smiled with satisfaction upon hearing his last words. The latter, looking at his watch, said:

"There is no more, gentlemen. Within a few hours you will receive specific individual orders and in a sealed envelope. They can retreat to their bases.

The chiefs who were there got up from their seats and, making isolated comments, left the room. Eisenhower was left alone inside the room, he contemplated in silence the map that was spread out before him and smiled, with satisfaction. He lit a cigarette and remained motionless for a few seconds. Then he headed for the exit as well. The cool night air greeted those who came out of the interior of that little house. The engines of the military cars started up, they roared, the headlights came on , tearing through the darkness, and the cars, along the winding road, moved away from the building. The military car of the RAF, ran dizzyingly, leaving behind a thick cloud of dust. Bumping over the rough road, the car was getting closer to its base in Tobruk. In the distance could be seen the lights of the African city. In the silence of the night, the roar of the engine seemed to intensify. Inside the car, its occupants wanted to get to the base, and end this annoying trip. Colonel Burton, head of the Tobruk air base, was a man of few words, tall and strongly built, looking younger than his years. His slightly graying blond hair contrasted against the reddish brown of his face. His light eyes, likewise, stood out enormously against the color of his skin. The fingers of his long and spatulate hands demonstrated the manual dexterity with which he was endowed. With a frown, he was silent in the back seat of the car that was taking him to the base. In reality , the driver did everything possible to avoid the large and abundant potholes, without being able to avoid, catch one or another. All the way the colonel opened his mouth. He seemed to be in deep and interesting meditations. Only towards the end did he comment:

"This road is very bad.

The driver, hearing the comment made by the colonel, answered somewhat astonished:

" Yes sir, it is, I do my best to avoid potholes, but they are so close together that...

Making a gesture with his hand, the colonel interrupted the driver saying:

Well, I don't say anything to you.

"Thank you.

The journey continued without another word being heard from inside the car. Dawn was breaking when the car rolled on the tracks of the field, towards the dependencies of the same.

CHAPTER II

THE PLAN IS UNVEILED

The pilot when he does not fly, feels uncomfortable and restless crawling on the ground, When the poison of flight enters the blood of a man, he is continually drawn towards the open spaces by an indefinable force. Flying, becomes almost a necessity for the pilot, when nostalgia and bitterness take over the man who for major reasons is unable to fly.

It was known that a new action was being prepared. The base pilots were nervous as well as anxious to begin the action that seemed to be studied. It had been several days since there had really been any serious intervention, or any important flight, and that was enough cause for the pilots, accustomed to continuous action, to be dissatisfied. But the news that a new and important military action was planned was enough for spirits to rise and manifest anxiety to appear on the faces of the pilots. Positively and unofficially, nothing certain was known, however, "when the river sounds, it carries water", and the pilots knew it.

The sun beat down on the field, and the reflection was scorching. The green bushes were discolored and dried very quickly in that exhausting sun. Shelter from him in the wooden and corrugated barracks, the pilots of the Tobruk base commented and speculated on what was to come.

"Gentlemen, the time has come to loosen our limbs, by which I mean that hours of struggle and combat are approaching.

There was a murmur of concern as well as approval from the assembled.

"A long series of flights are upon us" the colonel continued "as a reward for the long and almost lethargic rest that we have enjoyed. We must launch our aircraft in a continual bombardment of the Channel Islands of Sicily. The High Command has decided to conquer Sicily, but to reach it it is absolutely necessary to start with the conquest of the islands of Pantelleria, Lampedusa and Linosa, which in reality, as you can understand, are the bridgeheads, necessary by force.

A gesture of unanimous approval reached the colonel, who felt satisfied with his men.

"We will initiate a total devastation of all defenses, both coastal and interior, of the three islands. We with our devices have to carry out our work with perfect purpose. The flights will begin tomorrow morning at five in the morning. To do this, the second and third bombing squadrons, protected by two battle groups of Hurricanes , will leave fully equipped for the mission.

The colonel's last words were received with great enthusiasm by those gathered. Those men were actually eager to fight for their principles and their ideals, the nerve of war was reflected in them.

"Any questions?

No one made the slightest sign of wanting to ask anything. The colonel, wiping his perspiring forehead with a handkerchief, ended by saying:

"At half past three in the morning the leaders of the squads I have mentioned will meet me right here. Nothing more.

Major Charles Cameron was walking slowly to his room, when he heard footsteps behind him and a voice, which he immediately recognized as the colonel's, saying:

"I wish to speak with you, Major.

Turning and waving, Cameron replied:

" At your disposal, sir.

With a gesture, the colonel indicated to the Major that he should continue walking down the corridor, heading for the officers' exit, where there was a small bar. Once in that room, the colonel, staring at the Major, said:

"I have a lot of confidence in you, Cameron.

"Thank my Lord.

Lighting a cigarette and offering another to the Major, the colonel continued.

"We started a stage of hard work, and I personally wish him the best of luck. I don't think it's actually very difficult to occupy these three little islands. However , it is always good to wish us luck, and I repeat, I wish it to you.

Through clenched teeth as if somewhat embarrassed by the colonel's words, the Major replied:

"I thank you for your words.

"You are the man who deserves the greatest confidence in me, of those who are here. You have fought several times under my command: and I know your fiber. I know it's tough. I entrust complete command of the mission to you.

"Thank you.

"Don't give them to me. Perhaps it will lead to his death.

"Or maybe to glory.

Both men stood staring at each other, as if expecting a sudden reaction. Lowering his eyes, the elder said:

"I hope I don't disappoint you, sir.

"I know he won't.

The wall clock counted the hours, with chilling march. The older Cameron glanced at him from time to time, as if expecting something, and in fact he was.

"He is nervous? asked the colonel.

" I don't know what to tell you. Thinking about what is coming I will tell you that I am a little nervous, it is not because of the fights that I will have to face; rather it is for fear of that trust that you have placed in me.

"Why?

"If I failed, it would be a very big blow, from a moral point of view. It would affect me more than you can imagine.

"Don't take it that way, Major," the colonel said in a consoling tone, continuing.

"You are a great aviator. We all know it and you should know it too. That will give him self-confidence, which is the greatest of all incentives, when we have to deal with cases like this one.

"I know, though...

"Nothing, Major, I do not allow you to hesitate in any way.

"Good.

"Now you must retire to sleep for a few hours. Few actually, because it does not have many. Go rest your nerves.

"Thank my Lord.

Rising from the comfortable armchair where he was sitting, he greeted his colonel and slowly walked toward the exit. Upon reaching it, he seemed to hesitate for a moment, but then with a firm hand he opened the door leaving the room. The colonel watched him leave, watching his every move.

Charles Cameron, lying on his bed thought about his school years, which were already behind him. At that time he was thirty years old and his military life was full of glory; however, deep inside there was something that did not let him be happy. The clock kept ticking. The shadows of the night were going to be broken by the light of dawn. In full flight gear, the Major went in search of specific orders.

CHAPTER III

ALARM

The always unpleasant fog prevented complete visibility. The British aircraft were flying in perfect formation in the direction of the predetermined objective. In the center of it the bombing devices were placed and covering these the fighters flew. Barely a quarter of an hour had passed since they had left the Africa base and were heading for the islands where they were to drop their deadly charges. Apart from the fog that clouded the atmosphere, the day was perfect for the flight. A slight headwind had allowed the aircraft to reach a respectable height. Majestic, the planes flew maintaining radio communication. Beneath them, the sea stretched out, perfectly calm, the light of the rising sun sparkling on its surface. Little by little, the mist was left behind, and the blue sky took on an exuberant sharpness. In the distance, the silhouettes of targets appeared on the horizon. Towards them the apparatuses were directed . Major Cameron was facing the enemy again, his sinewy hands gripping the command post, his feet bracing on the rudder pedals. His apparatus in the head directed the operation.

" Attentive to the chopped; slip to the right. Ten seconds!

Ten, nine, eight, seven, six, the seconds ticked by and the bombardment group was preparing to launch...

Zero...!

... the planes lined up their bows, on the targets spread out below them diving swiftly. The altimeters descended unanimously, while the earth seemed to be approaching the devices. Suddenly, the antiaircraft batteries of the island that was attacked, opened fire on them. It was to be expected that the Italian defenses would act. However, the island was more heavily defended than was actually believed. The anti-aircraft units fired very rapidly, so for a moment the British were taken aback. From the black bellies of the British planes came the deadly bombs. With a chilling hiss, they fell obliquely to the ground. The explosions followed one another. Cameron gained altitude and behind him the remaining bombers. Again the devices were ready to launch themselves on the targets. However, in front of them suddenly appeared an abundant formation of enemy hunting devices. The fight promised to be stronger than expected.

«... I have confidence in you, I have confidence in you...». The colonel's words hammered at Major Charles Cameron's temples.

The British fighters, the Hurricanes , attacked the enemy planes with deadly force. The devices of both sides chased each other in a terrible chase, leaving those hit with black trails of smoke in space. The bomber planes, ignoring as much as possible the presence of the enemy fighters, continued their stubborn bombardment, while the Hurricanes dealt with the fighters. The fire from the shore batteries had almost ceased as the Italian fighters appeared. Hell was in heaven. An English bomber struck by Italian fire exploded in mid-air, its flaming wreckage falling to the crushed earth of the island. The pilots unfortunately died. With a fixed, expressionless gaze, Cameron followed the trajectory of the remains of the compatriot plane. The machine guns of both sides did not stop singing their macabre songs, the lead spat by them, furrowed the spaces in all directions, filling everything with death and terror. The fighting between the fighters was bloodthirsty, but noble. The devices rushed each other and when they were at a certain distance they fired their weapons. The pilots made truly master flights to avoid being hit by the gusts. The tracer bullets looked like ghosts chasing the chosen enemy. Major Cameron, terminated the performance, when the bomb reserves had been exhausted, then ordered the return to base.

The Italian planes stubbornly pursued the RAF aircraft. The British fighters rabidly attacked the pursuers. Lifting his goggles and loosening his seat belt a bit, the major said to his second, stationed in the rear cockpit.

"It hasn't been bad to begin with.

The second, looking up from the dashboard and nodding to the elder, replied:

"Not much less, it has been forecast. I did not expect the Italians to welcome us with such energy.

"Nor I...

Suddenly the second called out to the mayar.

"We lose fuel!

Sure enough, the fuel gauge needle dropped dangerously.

"We have a tailwind. We will arrive, I am sure, if the atmospheric conditions do not change.

The second pilot, making a gesture of doubt answered the major.

"We will see.

"Don't hesitate.

The apparatus continued to fly at a steady pace. The tailwind seemed to intensify and at the same time the loss of fuel seemed to have stopped. The oldest, turning to the second, said:

" Everything is going well, we will arrive.

"So it seems. The tailwind gives us a great advantage.

"Of course.

In the distance the contours of the African coast began to be distinguished. Joy flooded the hearts of the airmen. Cameron took a deep breath. His plane was holding up and he had no doubt then that he would reach the Tobruk base.

The engine was beginning to misfire as Major Charles Cameron flew over the base. However , he no longer had any fear; was flying over the airfield.

"We are saved! the eldest shouted, turning to his second.

"Yes, I do not deny that I was afraid of not arriving.

"But down there is our solid ground. I'm going to land. Hold on. The aircraft began to lose height heading towards the ground in somewhat tilted flight. After a few moments of anguish, Cameron righted the plane, dropping to the ground in a perfect three-point shot. The plane rolled across the ground heading toward the hangars. After the apparatus of the largest followed the others landing in perfect order all of them.

"Ready" said the major, getting out of the cockpit and taking off his flight helmet.

"Thank God" the second commented behind his back.

"Give the opportune orders to review the apparatus.

"Good.

"Give me in a few minutes an account of the losses and the damage suffered in the other devices.

"Yes sir.

"Make it exact.

"Good.

With a determined step, the major went to the colonel's office, with the intention of giving an account of everything that had happened. During the tour of the short space that separated him from the office, a multitude of ideas came to his head. "I am not a failure. I have not disappointed the colonel.' Actually , the older Cameron had never been a failure, however he was never happy with himself, everything he did seemed little and worthless . He stopped for a few moments in front of the office door, thought about what expression he would give to his face, and then decidedly entered. The Colonel's gaze fixed on him. At times he felt an anguished anguish.

"At your service Mr.

Getting up the colonel asked.

"What's new?

CHAPTER IV

THE COMMENTS

The bar at Tobruk air base was packed with pilots and officers discussing the intervention that had been carried out over the Sicilian channel islands. admiration.

"The Italians were prepared: How did they know our offense? Very strange things happen; I assure you.

A young pilot, perhaps the youngest of all those who were there, who, due to the decorations that covered his chest, seemed to be a true air navigation ace, answered:

"It was the most logical and natural thing. They knew that in a few hours of flight, leaving from Tobruk, we were on them, so they had to be prepared and...

"I disagree" interrupted the old pilot, continuing. The high command had informed us that the Italians were completely unprepared.

"But things usually happen the way you least expect it.

"What do you mean?

"Well, that, we can't trust anyone in the slightest.

"Why?

"The Italians, of course, will have their information service.

Those gathered will remain silent for a few moments as if studying the last words of the young aviator. He looked at his companions, and suddenly the doubt arose in him as to whether perhaps he had offended them with his words.

" I think you will understand my words" he warned in a somewhat submissive tone of voice. His companions smiled at him and one of them patted him on the back and replied:

"Friend, it seems to me that you read too many gory novels.

They all laughed and the aforementioned answered.

"It's been a long time since I've read crime novels, but I won't deny that I used to read as many as I could get my hands on. Some of them are very interesting and one gets distracted for little money, and...

An officer approaching the speaker interrupted him saying:

"Listen, Powell, you don't need to explain it to us, but we already know your great ability to read and all that stuff, which if I remember correctly you've explained to us at least a couple of hundred times.

Somewhat embarrassed, Powell looked up and stared over his partner's shoulder at Major Charles Cameron, who smiled at him at the puzzled look on his face.

"Will you shut me up?

"It's not that, what we don't want is for you to repeat the album.

"Well, then I'm leaving.

Taking his cap, the pilot Powell began to walk away from the group formed by his companions, who laughed at his good-natured appearance. Major Cameron approaching Captain Leith said:

"He really is a good boy.

Turning the captain towards whom he was speaking, he replied in a tone of affirmation.

"Yes, sir, it is.

"I think they mess with him too much.

"You believe?

"Yes.

"I will try to fix it.

Cameron took another sip from his glass of beer and then looked at the group of pilots in silence for a few moments. The aviators talked about the most diverse topics, almost continuously changing the conversation of shades and colors. One of the topics that was most often exploited was talking about the past, about the homes they had left, the family that was far away, the girlfriends and friends they wanted to see. Everyone was passionate about the subject, and generally, almost for a rigorous turn, the aviators explained their lives, almost with hair and ink.

"... That is my life...

"Very vulgar," replied Captain Leith to a lieutenant who had just recounted some of the facts of what he called "his hectic life."

"There's nothing vulgar about it," he replied somewhat offended to the captain's reply.

Meant to anger him, Leith did not change his mind.

"I find nothing in her that is worth mentioning.

"He does it on purpose to piss me off, doesn't he?

"None of that, I give you my most sincere opinion.

The aviators smiled at the companion's irritability. Captain Leith seemed amused.

Around eight at night, the base bar was closed, forcing all the aviators to vacate it. With a gesture of displeasure they went out. Major Cameron had long since left, leaving his companions lost in the explanations of their respective lives. The night was clear; perhaps in excess. The full moon appeared as a large disk suspended in space. None of the pilots liked that light, it was ideal to suffer a night attack. Captain Leith, after lighting a cigarette, leaned against the window sill, watching the landing field spread out before him. Suddenly he felt someone ask him from behind.

" Worried?

The captain turned to see who was speaking to him and recognized his partner, Captain Sammy Geldon .

"Nope.

"Thinking?

"Something like that.

Geldon looked at his companion with some curiosity, and without being able to help it, he asked.

"What are you thinking about?

Leith without looking at who was asking and in a low voice answered.

"On Major Cameron.

"In the eldest! Why?

"I would like to know what he is hiding in his previous life, I mean before he moved. All of us have explained his life countless times, and we all know what we have done to date, but he, if you notice, keeps his past hidden.

"You are somewhat right, but he told us that he was an archaeologist.

"But nothing else...

Leith took a few long drags, then let two wisps of smoke escape from his nose.

"And what do you care about the older man's past?

"It's not that I'm really worried, it's that I'm curious to know what it doesn't explain; to know his life.

"Perhaps the day you least expect it, he will release all the stuff of his life and then you will be disappointed.

"Can be.

"You can almost be sure of it.

"I would be glad if it were.

The two officers began to walk side by side, heading to their assigned bedrooms. Geldon looking at the sky and making a gesture of concern said:

"It would not be difficult for us to have a visitor tonight.

" It could be, but it is better not to think.

"Certain.

"Good evening, and don't create a scary novel around the elder.

"I will, good night.

"Bye.

CHAPTER V

MORE ANNOUNCEMENTS

Red with fire, the sun rose, waking up the day with its clear lights, illuminating the space. The sky was completely clear and a light wind from the North tended to lower the ambient temperature. Not the slightest movement was observed on the airfield, it seemed as if everything was still asleep, but in reality, a feverish activity had been going on for two hours, hidden under the covers of the hangars and outbuildings. The night had passed calmly, without anything disturbing the peace at all, during that period of time when the day star is hidden from the gaze of men. The blowing wind raised with its gusts, small amounts of sand and earth, which moved, through the airfield, crashing against the walls of the hangars. Bushes dried by the sun were likewise dragged by the wind, in a continuous coming and going. In the atmosphere there was something of desolation; something like a shade of sadness seemed to have passed that morning over the Tobruk airfield. The sleeve indicated the direction of the wind, at the top of the meteorological tower suffering deviations from time to time. Everything, in fact, was monotonous and heavy. The planes, like great dead monsters, remained motionless inside the hangars, as if paralyzed by the sadness of that dawn. However , as the sun rose, the most insignificant objects seemed to come to life, bathing little by little everything in the colors of life.

Inside the conference room, there were a large number of pilot officers, who were grouped together holding different conversations while waiting for the arrival of the Base Chief, Colonel Burton, who had ordered them to meet for an interview. The aviators asked each other, what would be the reason that originated that one, meeting. They would have been waiting approximately twelve minutes, when Colonel Burton suddenly appeared before them, who, addressing them, said:

"Sit down, gentlemen.

Obeying what was ordered, the aviators chose a site and settled down. Moments later, an almost sepulchral silence reigned, which was broken by the colonel's thick and manly voice.

"Actually, it is not that I have great things to say to you, however I wanted to have an exchange of impressions with you.

The aviators looked at each other, in mute questions. The colonel continued:

"In our attack on the island of Pantelleria, we were surprised by strong enemy opposition that we did not expect. True, it was to be expected that the Italians would defend themselves, but the way they did, no. Apparently the three islands are well prepared, to stop our attacks, right? "Unanimous approval rose from the assembled pilots." Not only has the strong and tough defense of the anti-aircraft guns amazed us, but also the intervention of enemy aircraft, with which we did not really count, from which it can be deduced that the mission that has been entrusted to us, It is not as easy or simple as it seemed to be at first. On the contrary , it presents serious difficulties. However , counting on your expertise, I know that we will be victorious in our mission. My words are not to encourage you, for I know there is no need for it. I'm just giving you the facts.

The colonel's voice, calm and even, without highs or lows, had a pleasant tone. Those gathered listened with growing interest to the colonel's words, who, looking alternately at everyone, explained his plans and projects. The room was actually small to accommodate that fairly large number of aviators, some of whom had to sit on extra beds.

"Given the experience we have had" the colonel continued, "it is necessary that in the next interventions we tread more carefully or rather, that we act with greater mischief. Today we will not make any flights. However , at midnight you will take off in order to carry out the bombardment in the early hours of dawn, during which without any doubt, the defense servants will be more unprepared, do you understand?

The colonel's question was actually completely unnecessary, since what he had stated did not contain anything out of the ordinary and difficult to understand, but it was his custom to always ask at the end of each point, however simple it might be. Those gathered already knowing this particularity, they nodded almost mechanically, before which the colonel felt satisfied and encouraged to continue the exposition of facts. After a moment's silence, he spoke again.

"This time the expedition will be made up of the same devices as the previous one, adding one more squadron of fighters, which are always useful and necessary. In this way the bombing apparatus itself will be able to act with more freedom than before, even though there is strong Italian opposition.

The idea that one more squadron of Hurricanes would be added , in that incursion that was to be carried out, seemed to please the pilots of the bombing devices, because a wide smile was reflected on their faces, which proved it. Colonel Burton knew that his idea had been welcomed by his pilots and was somewhat pleased with it.

"Do you want to ask me any questions? the colonel finished.

Gardiner , suddenly rose and asked:

"Our goal: is it exactly the same as last time?

Mockingly smiling complacently answered.

" Yes, the same, anything else?

"Yes.

"I asked for.

"Should we maintain radio contact with the base?

"No, not at all, they should completely forget about the existence of radio.

"Understood.

"I will not give them new orders, because they already know what they must do. You may now withdraw, and rest for the time remaining to you.

"Thank you.

The pilot officers left the room heading to their rooms. Major Charles Cameron quietly as usual headed for his bedroom when he felt his name called. He immediately recognized the voice of Captain Gardiner , who, approaching, asked him.

"What's wrong? I find you worried.

As there was a certain friendship between the major and the captain, no one was surprised that the captain had called the major, in a truly friendly way.

"I'm not well.

"But I seem to guess there is something bothering you...

"You're wrong. You fail as a psychologist.

"Fine, I give up.

Extending his hand to the captain, the Major said:

"Let's go, we must rest. Tomorrow a bone awaits us.

"You're right, good night.

"Bye.

Cameron went into his room and lay down on the bed without undressing. Moments later, he was fast asleep.

CHAPTER VI

NEW ENCOUNTER

The devices appeared as small specks in the infinite blue night. The stars twinkled and the moon with its silver light bathed the devices that , at more than three thousand meters high, crossed the open space like an infinite abyss. The RAF squadrons, in high-altitude flight, were heading for the objective that had been pointed out to them. The devices in perfect formation, roaring their engines at maximum force, glided swiftly over the fillets of air. The aerodynamic lines of the planes cut through the air, almost without resistance, within the technical limits reached. Above the aviators was the magnificent spectacle of the night devoid of clouds and curdled with countless stars led by the star of the night.

Below, deep down, the sea felt solid, hard and cold as steel. The moonlight sparkled on the surface of the waters with metallic reflections, like mercury. The propellers of the airplanes twisted in the air, expelling it backwards, and forcing the mass of steel and iron to remain in the air, neglecting the effect of gravity. Moonlight streamed into the cockpits, giving the aviators the look of mummies. The illuminated control panel showed the pilot the flight situation and its conditions. The night was the protection of that flight that the English carried out on the Italian bases of the islands of the channel of Sicily.

When the aircraft took off from the air base, Colonel Burton remained in his office observing the aircraft's takeoff maneuvers through the glass of one of the windows . Satisfied , he watched them take off, while a pleased smile appeared on his face. He had faith in his men and knew that they were fighting tooth and nail for the maintenance of their ideals. The last rumblings of the engines had already faded in the distance, when the somewhat tired colonel lay down on his bed, looked at his watch and, taking a deep sigh, tried to sleep, seeing in his imagination the silhouette of the planes moving in search of of the enemy. The tick tock of the clock seemed to have increased in volume becoming a heavy hammering, sleep did not come and the nerves were taking over the colonel who impatiently consulted the clock with terrible frequency.

In their monotonous flight the devices were getting closer to the indicated objective. Major Cameron completely calm communicated with his co-pilot.

"Go over the weapons, and accessories.

"Well sir.

"In a few minutes, we'll be over our point. The time to act will have come again.

"I know.

Cameron fixed his sight on the horizon. Suddenly her heart skipped a beat. There in the distance, he had seemed to distinguish some bright points. Could they be enemy planes? He fixed his eyes and paid more attention. After a few moments of hesitation, he saw again those tiny points that were approximately at the same height as them. Nervous, he informed the copilot of the observation made. He looked where the elder indicated.

"I don't distinguish...

"Take a good look...

For a few moments a terrible nervous tension reigned.

"Yes, now I see them...!

"What do you think...?

The co-pilot took a few moments to reply. Then with an affirmative intonation he answered.

" They are planes and they are coming here.

"There is not the slightest doubt. They are Italian. It will communicate it to the other devices.

Very quickly, the major communicated to the apparatuses that formed the forces that were going to Pantelleria, the presence of apparently enemy planes. Once the observation was notified, the bombers gained altitude and the fighter aircraft headed for the points that had appeared on the horizon and that were gradually gaining in size, being able to distinguish the silhouette of the enemy planes perfectly moments later.

"The fighters will take care of them, we dispense with it and go directly to our objective" said the major to his second.

"Good.

"These are the orders we have.

"I know.

"Anyway, pay attention, as is natural, the Italian fighters are coming for us more than for the Hurricanes , they are interested in us because we are the big bird.

"It is the most natural.

"Presto.

The combat that was approaching them promised to be somewhat stronger than the previous one since on this occasion, both sides increased the number of planes. The English had added a hunting squadron, and the enemy forces, at first glance, seemed more numerous than the previous time. The Italian aircraft, making a rapid maneuver in unison, turned onto their side, attacking the RAF planes from the side.

"He was armed! the older shouted to his second.

"And it promises to be a relief.

"Let's gain more height, it suits us.

"Yes sir.

"Up!

Pulling briskly on the control post, Major Cameron raised his craft to greater heights, out of the fire of the Italian fighters.

"There is the island! "The second shouted, pointing to a black mass that extended over the sea.

"Yes, when we are on it, we will sting.

"And the other gadgets?

"They will do the same.

The Hurricanes clashed with the enemy aircraft, in a bloody rush. The machine guns spoke, and in space the tracer bullets left white trajectories headed by a point of light. Both the pilots of one side and the other, proved to be men of great courage since they fought with great contempt and courage. When making a slip on the left wing, a Hurricane to get out of the area of fire of an enemy plane, which was shooting at it head-on, an Italian aircraft crossed it, producing the inevitable cataclysm. Both planes were embedded one inside the other, and the two united by the flames, rushed into the void, dragging the pilots. Moments later the sea engulfed the flaming mass.

When Cameron dived over the island, heading to the places indicated as targets on the island, he was preceded by the rest of the bombing apparatus. All as one they were approaching the island in a vertiginous fall while the Italian fighters made real efforts to prevent it. The bombs fell from the interior of the devices and these, describing a deadly trajectory, collided with the ground of the island. The explosions of the innumerable bombs filled the space with red flashes and black smoke. Suddenly a great flame rose high above the island floor.

"We have touched a gas tank!

Major Cameron answered his second with a terse nod. The flames of the fire rose menacingly, crowned by thick black smoke. The sun was rising, when the island was left over, several important fires could be observed, the result of the bombardment by British aviation.

CHAPTER VII

RESTLESSNESS

What time would it be? When Colonel Burton awoke with a start , he was completely unaware whether he had slept much or little. The first thing he noticed was that the dawn sun was coming in through the office window. Then suddenly he became aware of the classic roar of aircraft engines. They were back! When he stepped outside the cool dawn air blew into his face, comforting Colonel Burton. To the Northeast could be seen the perfect formations of the English aircraft returning from the mission they had accomplished. Burton ordered a cup of hot coffee, which he had drunk in a few minutes.

The aircraft began to touch down, in perfect shots, with the exception of one bomber whose landing gear was in poor condition, stuck its nose into the ground, breaking its propellers and its right wing. Apart from this accident, the shots were otherwise masters. With relief, the colonel was able to verify that almost all the devices were returning, more than he actually believed.

Major Cameron, haggard from the stress of the operation, was sipping a cognac, while the colonel looked at him with a questioning expression.

"That's right, colonel" said the major after finishing the cognac.

"What you tell me is amazing.

With great attention the colonel had listened to the detailed narration and exposition of facts made by Major Cameron, of the encounter with the enemy planes.

"How many Italian aircraft made up the defense?

"Ten more than us.

" It will be a matter of putting the high command up to date on what happened. Apparently the Italian forces receive information about our movements and displacements.

"That's right, sir. I assure you that my surprise knew no bounds when I saw the enemy aircraft appear in a straight line above us.

"How many Italian planes did they manage to shoot down?

"Twelve, sir.

"Good number.

"Yes, sir, especially considering that we only lost three planes and two of them fighters.

"It's a good difference.

"It is a victory.

"Okay, it is. However , the fact that the enemy planes were waiting for them somewhat clouds that victory. Not from the active point of view in combat, but in the organization plan.

"I don't understand.

"It's very simple" the colonel clarified, "I mean that among us there is someone who informs the Italians, and that is a failure of the security department.

"I don't see it very feasible.

"Why?

"We know each other very well, and I would dare to put my hands in the fire for all of them...

"And it would burn" the colonel energetically interrupted.

"Means?

"I am completely sure.

For a few moments there was an awkward silence, the two men looked at each other, saying nothing. Suddenly the colonel, giving a furious punch, exclaimed:

"Yes, it would burn!

Major Cameron observing the state of the colonel did not dare to make the slightest comment.

He remained silent, while he smoked very slowly a cigarette that he had lit.

When the major left the colonel's office he felt depressed without being able to define the just and exact reason. He fell on his bed and his mind wandered remembering the most intense moments of the fight, which he had held hours ago. Little by little the fatigue gave him over, the images became more confused until they faded completely and he fell asleep.

The sun let its heat be felt, falling perpendicularly on the airfield. Inside the hangars the temperature was suffocating to the extreme, the reverberation that rose from the field made the atmosphere practically unbreathable, which at that time was endowed with the most complete immobility. That sun was truly capable of putting anyone to sleep. Everything was impregnated in a lethargic prostration. The airfield was limited to the south by a road in very poor conditions, to the north its buildings and another road, to the east some large depressions in the land ended the field and to the west, the city of Tobruk. The coastal artillery pieces anxiously looked towards the sea, waiting for the enemy squad, the city itself was well defended being all of it surrounded by wide and deep trenches, pillboxes and machine gun nests, as well as a strong defense garrison .

Around five in the afternoon Major Cameron awoke from his deep sleep, feeling more comforted and with greater energy, getting up, lighting a cigarette and looking through the windows at the wide panorama of the airfield. A faint smile seemed to appear on his face for a few moments, he adjusted his tie and left his room. In the officers' room there were a large number of them, entertaining themselves in the most diverse games, Cameron looked at those gathered as if looking for someone determined. However , what he was looking for was a quiet corner. He saw an empty table and went to it, sat down and began to leaf through a French magazine.

Cigarette smoke accumulated on the ceiling of the room. The pilots talked and talked nonchalantly, giving their opinions on recent events. Major Cameron, engrossed in his reading, seemed not to hear what was being said. He stood for half an hour or so without looking up from the magazine. Then he put it down, laced his fingers together and let them rest on his legs, tilted his head back and was thoughtful. Someone broke the chain of his imagination by asking:

"Is she blonde?

Looking up, the older man saw his friend Gordon.

"I don't understand" he clarified as if coming out of semiconsciousness.

"I ask you if that girl you were thinking of is blonde.

"And who told you that I was thinking of a girl?

"You just had to see the face you had.

"And how was it?

"Silly.

"Thank you.

"Don't be angry, but a man can only make that face when he thinks of a woman. If you had seen yourself in a mirror, you would have been ashamed.

"Well, you're wrong, I didn't think of any woman, and besides, I don't think I had a stupid face.

Sitting next to his partner, Gordon said quietly.

"I am also worried. I also think that the Italians receive information from someone who is perhaps in this very room.

"Again I ask you, and who told you that I was thinking about that?

" Very simple, the colonel has told me the same thing as you, what he thinks, and I know that your concern is the words of the colonel, which are mine too.

"You're right.

"And who can it be?

"I do not know.

"It is unpleasant.

"Yes, very much" replied the eldest, getting up from the chair, and leaving his friend alone.

CHAPTER VIII

WHO WILL IT BE?

The new Hurricanes evolved perfectly in free space, over the Tobruk field. The test was being observed by its commanders, who were amazed at the great mobility of the new devices. The clean and perfect silhouette of the planes stood out majestically against the blue of the sky.

"Wonderful gadgets," the colonel told the head of security, Major Wayne.

"Indeed they are.

"Nor can we complain about the drivers, who drive them. All of them prove to be true aces.

As they spoke, neither of the two leaders took their eyes off the planes that were following their test flight, doing a great number of stunts and stunts. The test flight lasted nearly half an hour, after which Colonel Burton gave the order for the aircraft to land.

"Now it is OK. They've already shone enough. Let them land "said the colonel with some severity to a lieutenant who was a short distance from him. When the officer received the order, he ran to the control tower, from which the pilots were told to carry out the landing. With great precision, keeping the distances in a mathematical way, the planes approached the ground until they landed.

"Good! exclaimed the colonel with satisfaction.

The head of security smiling heard the colonel's expression.

"Yes, magnificent.

"Now, Wayne, come to my office. I want to talk to you about a rather serious matter.

" Well, sir.

Followed by the major, the head of the base, he started walking towards his offices. The small figure of the head of security was materially overshadowed by the enormous body of his superior. With a somewhat slow step, Colonel Burton quietly entered his office. Once in it, he made a sign with his head, indicating the head of security to sit down, he silently did what he was told. The sun streamed in through the window and the temperature inside the office was a bit suffocating. Picking up the telephone receiver, Burton ordered them to bring him a couple of beers. The fact was a note of color, which cheered Major Wayne somewhat. He immediately understood that if his superior had made him go to his office, for a reprimand he would have suppressed that detail. Suddenly Burton without further ado said:

"You, like me, know that among our men there is one of them who informs the Italians.

So point blank, the comment was made that the head of security was somewhat taken aback. However , overcoming the first impression, he answered, concisely.

"Yes.

"Who?

"What more would I like than to answer that question, without hesitation of any kind, but unfortunately it cannot be. It is very difficult to make an accusation of that kind, without evidence.

Burton looked at his interlocutor with a certain expression of astonishment on his face. Then in doubt he said:

"It almost follows from your words that you suspect someone.

"Me...

At that moment there was a knock at the door of the office, and after receiving the appropriate authorization from the colonel, a soldier entered the room with the ordered beers. After leaving them where the colonel indicated, the soldier withdrew.

"What was he going to tell me? asked the colonel.

With some nervousness the head of security said:

"Really all men deserve complete security from us. Reviewing their war histories and their family backgrounds, we see that they are all magnificent warriors as well as members of good families when it comes to patriotism, but...

"But what?

"You see, there is one of them whose past appears mired in certain mists and who is known to have studied in the capital of Italy.

"Who?

Looking closely at the colonel's face, the Security Chief said:

"Major Charles Cameron.

The silence became crushing. The colonel fixed his eyes on who had mentioned the Major. Then, turning his back, he said almost furiously:

"Impossible!!

"Nothing is impossible, sir.

"If you allow me, I will ask you, why?

In a very quick turn, the colonel turned to the person who was formulating such a question. He looked at the latter for a few moments roughly, and then explained:

"I have known Major Cameron for a long time. I have seen him operate on many occasions and in all of them he has shown great courage, and a great sense of patriotism. He has been at death's door on several occasions and... Well, it can't be.

Nervously, Burton lit a cigarette, offering another to Major Wayne.

"However, sir, you had to take my observation into account.

"What does it mean?

With a nod of agreement, the Head of Security explained:

" All of our drivers show a great sense of rapport. Everyone, before everyone, has explained their life and their most intimate actions and adventures many times. Have you noticed that the Major never talks about his past?

"Your reasons will have.

"That's what I say, his reasons will have . Why does he hide his past?

Burton remained silent, the expression on his face of a man tormented by an unpleasant idea. Then he exclaimed:

"No, and a thousand times no!, and discard that idea. Our man must be another, and now a question. Whoever it is, how does it transmit the information?

"That's no problem, today there are transmitters the size of a cookie jar. Our man may have one of these devices hidden.

"If we found the device, we would have the informant.

"Certain.

"Then look for the device! "The colonel almost screamed.

"I will, but we have to wait for a propitious moment. I mean a time when the pilots are flying; all of them, of course.

"That's easy to get.

"It's up to you.

"I know, you don't have to tell me.

The Security Chief understood that the colonel was highly irritated and decided to measure his words. He was silent until the colonel said:

"Would two hours of time be enough?

"Yes sir, rather, I think so.

"Well, then make your preparations.

"What hours will those be?

"From seven to nine in the morning.

"Good.

" Now you can retire.

"Thank my Lord.

The head of security, getting up, saluted the colonel and, heading for the door, left the room.

was sinking on the horizon, when Colonel Burton left his office, with a frown and almost without answering the greetings of his subordinates, he went to the control tower, from which through the loudspeaker service, he spoke to their pilots.

CHAPTER IX

A TEST

Cameron did not understand the reason for this unexpected flight. They had been ordered out to sea, up to a certain point, and kept there in circular flight. Would an air attack be expected? Engines thundered through space as aircraft bobbed in the air. The day was crystal clear and therefore the visibility was perfect. Through the windows of the cockpits, the sun entered his nascent posture, caressing the aviator. The sea stretched out below the pilots like an immaculate blue sheet, dotted with flashes of light, with not the slightest trace of life visible as far as the eye could see. With his goggles up and his helmet loose, Cameron turned to say to his co-pilot:

"What do you think?

"Frankly I don't know, when they have made us leave for something it will be. However , everything is very quiet.

"That is what I say.

"Perhaps it was a false alarm.

"Who knows, we will fly for the indicated time and then we will return to the base.

"Good.

"Take the controls.

"Yes sir.

Obeying the copilot took the controls of the device. Then, removing his helmet, the Major opened the cockpit a crack and filled his lungs with the fresh morning air at eight thousand feet above sea level.

"How long have we been flying? asked the Major.

"One hour and seven minutes.

" I want to go back to base and take a good shower. One hour under cold water, very cold.

"I understand you.

Actually inside the cockpit one was sweating copiously, despite all the technical advances. The heat from the engine raised the temperature inside the device to exaggeration.

While the aircraft were flying in full, a strange maneuver was taking place at the Tobruk base. The head of Security, with some of his men, toured the pilots' bedrooms, materially searching every corner of them. When: they made sure that there was nothing in sight that could raise suspicions, the Major ordered that they go through all the pilots' bags. One by one, the order was carried out and carried out.

"We still have half an hour left" warned the Security Chief to his second who was nervously checking his watch.

"I know, but what if they came back earlier?

"Bad luck.

"We would raise suspicions and whoever it was would refrain from acting, misleading us.

"Don't worry. They have an order and they will carry it out. We are guaranteed the half hour.

"Better.

"Of course.

The suitcase corresponding to Major Cameron was, like all others, open.

"I am very interested in checking that suitcase myself," exclaimed the eldest, heading towards said suitcase, which one of his men had taken.

Placing the suitcase on the bed, he proceeded to open it. With an anxious gaze, he observed what was inside of it. With great care, without altering the order of placement, he searched. Suddenly he found some papers, which were hidden at the bottom of the suitcase. Wayne walked over with the papers in the light from the window looking at them. He could see that with a nervous hand he separated a paper that he read with interest. For a few moments he remained silent and motionless. Then calling his second he said:

"Read this.

The officer obeyed. Then he looked up, looked at his superior, and nodded understanding.

"What do you think?

"Interesting, sir.

"Yes a lot. I'll talk to the colonel. Now let's suspend the record. Put everything back in its place and clear the bedrooms.

"Well sir.

"You only have ten minutes.

"I know.

"Well quick.

After saluting, the officer left, returning the paper to the Chief of Security, who put it back in its place. He closed the suitcase and put it where it was before.

Colonel Burton stared at the Chief of Security. This perhaps felt annoyed under the inquisitive gaze of his superior; breaking the silence said:

"Yes, sir, perhaps I have obtained strong enough evidence to dispel your doubts as to Major Cameron.

"And what tests are those?

Giving himself some importance, with a certain air of superiority, Wayne explained:

"We have carried out the search as we had said, not finding anything suspicious, until in Major Cameron's suitcase, I myself found ...

"What did you find? the colonel asked nervously.

"One direction.

"One direction?

" Yes.

"And what do you want to prove with a simple address?

"It is that this direction is not so simple.

"By...?

"You see, the address is as follows, Gustavo Papinni , Dunaci , Pantelleria.

The security chief's words seemed to have no effect on the colonel, who, sitting down quietly and lighting a cigarette, said:

"With that address nothing is proven.

"Something if.

"And what is that something?

"That Major Cameron has unofficial contact with the island of Pantelleria.

"That does not prove his guilt. There is nothing that prohibits you from having a friendship in Pantelleria.

Somewhat disconcerted by the colonel's continual rebuffs, the security chief fell silent. Then getting up he said:

"I just didn't like it. I'm pretty sure there's something behind the major.

"You can think what you want, but I need proof, do you understand? I need evidence and convincing, no assumptions or ramblings. Tests, tests.

The colonel was apparently in a state of great irritability, pacing from one side of the room to the other with his hands behind his back.

"In two days we will make another visit to the island; a new bombardment. I hope by then you can tell me who is to blame.

"I'll try.

"I know that it is not an easy task, but it must be fulfilled.

"Well sir.

"Now back off and forget about that address, got it?

" Yes, sir.

CHAPTER X

DOUBTS

After the time indicated by the command, the devices returned to the base. During the two-hour flight, not the slightest abnormality had been observed, so the aircraft returned just as they had taken off. The flight had been quiet and calm, something almost unknown to these men, accustomed to facing death every time they took off. In perfect formation the planes came roaring their engines over the airfield. Describing wide circles they began to lose height preparing to land. One by one the devices landed with ample mastery running along the field towards the hangars. A quarter of an hour later, all the planes were already resting with their muted engines on the grass of the field. The pilots descending from their devices went to take off their flight equipment, which was overwhelming and uncomfortable. Major Cameron, accompanied by his co-pilot, went to refresh the "nut," as he called it.

Almost in one go he drank the glass of foamy beer that had been left before him. After savoring it for a few seconds, Cameron commented.

"It's delicious.

"Yes, and more so after a boring two-hour flight.

Cameron's co-pilot, like Cameron, emptied his glass of beer in one sip.

When the eldest lay down on his bed , he felt restless, restless. For half an hour he lay there without being able to calm down. There was something unpleasant in the air that he couldn't quite define. Suddenly there was a knock at the door and a soldier came in and notified the major that the colonel was waiting for him in his office. Cameron was not surprised. I was unconsciously waiting for that call. Slowly he got up from the bed, and buttoning up his jacket, he left his room to go to his superior's office.

The colonel was friendly, perhaps more than ever, although it is true that he had always shown great appreciation for the major.

"Sit down, sit down...

"Thank you.

Offering the major a cigarette, the colonel lit another.

"Is the flight easy?

"Yes a lot.

"I supposed.

"I also.

The Major's reply surprised the Colonel, who asked point-blank:

"Why did I assume?

"Well, honestly, I don't know, but from the moment I took off I had the fixed idea that it would be nothing more than a walk.

"That's funny.

"Maybe.

Without further ado, the colonel asked:

"Do you know the island of Pantelleria?

Without showing the slightest surprise, the major coldly answered the question in the following terms:

"Yes, I was in it a few years ago.

"Interesting?

"I remember a lot about her. It is an island that exudes tranquility. Its inhabitants are peaceful people.

Laughing the colonel commented.

"It won't be now.

"Of course. Everything has changed.

Sitting face to face, the two soldiers continued to talk for a long time, almost without formalities or rules, rather they spoke like old comrades.

"Well, Major, from what you tell me, that island must have been a true paradise in peacetime.

"Yes, I assure you. It was.

"Was he long?

"Two years.

"He must have gone through it from end to end, right?

"Yes, the island really didn't have an inch of land that I hadn't stepped on.

After a cigarette they smoked another and another. A thick cloud of smoke had formed in the colonel's office. The sun was almost sinking below the horizon when the colonel, looking at his watch, said:

"Gee, how late it has gotten.

"That's right," replied the eldest, suddenly realizing that the sun was dying.

"Another day he will continue telling me wonders of that island.

"With pleasure.

"Maybe when the war is over we'll go on a little trip for her.

Clapping the Major on the back, the Colonel got up and went to a cupboard and took out a bottle of cognac. He poured two small glasses and, advancing one towards Cameron, said:

"Let us drink to the success of our company.

"Thank you.

"It's good cognac.

Draining the last drop of liquor, the major said:

"You're right, it's exquisite.

"It is, do you want another one?

"No, thanks.

"Okay, let's go outside.

The evening air had cooled the air a bit so it was actually nice outside.

When the major separated from the colonel, he was surprised at the perhaps exaggerated kindness of his superior. The night was clear and I didn't feel like going to sleep. Cameron walked for a long time among the hangars and other outbuildings in the field. Then, quite late at night, tired, he decided to retire.

Colonel Burton with cocked head stared at the head of security, who seemed to be somewhat dismayed. Burton, in a somewhat gravelly voice, said:

"I can assure you of Major Cameron's complete innocence.

"Me...

Without giving him time to speak, the colonel cut off the major.

"Yes, yes, you believed, but it is not true. I would put my hands in the fire for the eldest.

"There is no need to rush. People know how to lie, do you forget, sir?

The question asked by the head of security made the colonel's face show a grimace of annoyance.

"Are you determined that...?

"It's not that I'm stuck on anything. For me, because of the position I hold, everyone is a suspect until proven otherwise.

"I understand.

"That is why I suspect and suspect.

"It is understandable.

"Do you give me carte blanche to act?

"Yes, as long as I don't pick up the hunt.

"Don't worry.

Both soldiers looked at each other in silence. The head of security, making a move to leave, said:

"I will keep you informed of all my inquiries.

"That is your duty.

When the head of security had left the office, the colonel, taking a thick tome with red covers, sat down in a wicker chair preparing to read.

CHAPTER XI

A TEST

At the base there was a certain nervousness. It was known for certain that Colonel Burton had been summoned that morning by the Brigadier General. This implied some event of importance. The colonel had left at eight in the morning and it was half past eleven the same when he still hadn't returned. The minutes passed slowly even more when everyone waited with interest for the colonel's arrival to find out what was happening.

At about half past twelve the expected happened. The colonel's car arrived along the dusty highway followed by an abundant cloud of dust, which rose as the car passed. The vehicle stopped in front of the offices and the colonel unhurriedly got out of it. Those who were nearby were disappointed when they realized that the colonel's face did not reflect the slightest expression that could guide them. The head of the base, after dusting himself off with a certain gesture of displeasure, entered his office, locked himself in it, and remained inside for half an hour without giving the slightest sign of life. Thing that came to increase the nervousness of the men who were under his command.

After eating, the major was about to have coffee at the bar when they told him to report to the colonel's office.

Burton, with his hands crossed on his belly, spoke very slowly, as if he wanted to observe the effect of his words on the older man, who listened attentively to what was being explained to him.

"Those are the orders I have received directly from the general. I know that the mission is extremely risky, but to carry it out, a man like you is necessary, with your military capacity and patriotism.

"Thank my Lord.

" You don't have to give them to me.

Cameron smiled, and said:

"Your confidence in me flatters me.

"You'll be flying in one of those late-model Hurricanes they've sent us. They offer greater security than the rest of the devices we have, don't you think?

"Yes.

"Well, as I was telling you, the photographs that you have to take, they have to be of the military bases, of the island of Pantelleria, as close as possible to them and the best you can. He will fly alone, that will relieve him of responsibilities.

"Certain.

Burton spread out a plan of the island on the table and, pointing to various points, said:

"This is where the war bases that make up the defense of the island are, you must know this terrain, right?

"Yes, I know him.

"That's a big plus for you.

Major Cameron nodded, and asked:

"When do I have to leave?

"At four. It looks good?

"Yes, perfectly, also today is a very clear day, so the photographs have a lot of cattle.

Burton listened to the Major's words complacently.

"Do you have any suggestion? asked the colonel.

Cameron remained silent, then shook his head in the negative.

"In that case, you can start making preparations for the flight.

"Good.

When Cameron was about to leave, the colonel stopped him saying.

"One thing I forgot.

"Hello, sir.

" No one, absolutely no one, should know the reason for your flight and where you are going.

"Good.

"It is of the utmost importance that you say nothing.

While making a gesture of understanding, Cameron replied:

"In agreement.

Through the windowpanes the colonel saw the Major walk away. Once he had disappeared around a corner, he went to the telephone and, picking up the receiver, said:

"Have Major Wayne come" and then he hung up the phone again.

A few minutes later the insignificant figure of the major entered the office.

In a few words, Colonel Burton explained to the head of the security service the fact that he had entrusted a special mission to Major Cameron. It seemed to sit badly with Wayne, for rising like a spring from where he was sitting, he said:

"But how has such a delicate mission been entrusted to the major, when doubts rest on him, that he is a possible enemy informer?

Without being in the least disturbed, Colonel Burton said:

"I keep telling you that the Major deserves all my trust, but notice one thing, on this flight you don't really risk anything, more than a few photographs, which another good pilot could take again, and if he really were an enemy informer, we offer you an opportunity to stay with yours.

The colonel's words seemed to calm the head of the security service.

"If he doesn't come back we'll be rid of him, and you, sir, will be greatly disappointed.

"If he didn't come back, that's how it would be, but the Major will come back.

"God willing.

For a few moments there was silence, but suddenly Colonel Burton said:

"He will leave with one of the latest model devices that we have received, and with a perfected photography team, total that will go to fulfill his mission with the best material we have.

With a slightly unpleasant singsong of doubt, Wayne commented:

"Well, well, we'll see what happens.

"Do you insist...?

"No, I have already told you that I am not committed to anything, sir, only that I distrust everyone.

For a long time the two men continued the conversation, with some nervous tension on both sides.

The sun was beating down on the airfield, over which a suffocating calm reigned, layers of overheated air rising from the ground, which sometimes seemed to take the breath away of anyone unlucky enough to be involved in one of these layers. So great was the prevailing heat that the gasoline drums for the aircraft had had to be taken to makeshift cellars, or else protected from the heat by showers of water every half hour. The men of the auxiliary services of the field, walked from one place to another, wearing shorts and a campaign shirt as their only clothing, most of them having replaced their boots with sandals. When the light breeze from the sea entered the field, the temperature dropped considerably, becoming even pleasant, but on days like this, when not the slightest gust of air blew, the heat was really unbearable. In the midst of that waste of light and heat, Major Cameron's flight was being prepared. The device was being carefully reviewed and under the supervision of Cameron himself the cameras were being attached.

CHAPTER XII

WHAT WILL HAPPEN?

As the engine warmed up, Cameron watched the clear sky, in which there was not the slightest trace of clouds. The sun's rays passed through the clean atmosphere without difficulty of any kind. The propellers of the device sang their song of strength and the device resting on its landing gear trembled slightly waiting for the moment to ascend in search of the spaces. Major Cameron got on the plane, fastened his seat belt, closed the cockpit, and after putting on his flight helmet, he prepared to take off. With his hands he made the sign "out chocks" and the assistants left the aircraft in a position to start the race. With a steady hand and mathematical precision, Cameron was giving gas to the engine, which began to roar more frantically, the device began to move moving along the ground. Little by little he was winning the race, standing up from the tail. The rev counter indicated the number of them needed to be able to take off without fear of stalling. A yank on the control post starts the device on a vertiginous ascent. Like a bird, it moved away in space with great serenity and elegance of movement. The automatic compensator responsible for keeping the device in perfect flight position, worked wonderfully. The plane without giving the slightest pitch or roll movement was getting smaller in the immense blue.

The control tower communicated to the major the weather conditions along the route he had to cover. Notifying him that this was perfect for the flight along the entire route.

When about ten minutes after the major had taken off, he entered the office of Colonel Burton, the head of the security service. The colonel said as a single and brief greeting.

" That's it.

"Yes, that's it. Now we just have to wait.

"That's it.

Both lighting a cigarette, they sat down in their respective wicker chairs. Burton unbuttoned his tunic a bit so as to suffer less from the rigors of time. Observing the colonel's face, one could see in it a certain and weak expression of uneasiness, finely captured by the head of security, who refrained from making the slightest comment. Burton looked at his watch and, throwing his head back, seemed to want to fall asleep. In truth, though, all she wanted in those nervous moments was to avoid talking to Wayne. The thunder of the engine of the plane piloted by Cameron seemed still to be heard in space. However, he was already lost on the horizon, leaving him with nothing but the anxiety of his return.

The officers and other pilots of the base were somewhat surprised by that flight made by the major. All had tried to find out the cause of it, without obtaining the slightest detail about it. Questions and false answers spread from mouth to mouth with the speed of wildfire. Nobody knew anything for sure and the suppositions and affirmations contradicted each other in such a way that a veritable labyrinth of ideas was formed . Airmen loitered around the conning tower, waiting for it to find out something. But the servants of said dependency, completely incommunicado following orders of the colonel, could not inform in the least about Major Cameron. From time to time the colonel contacted the tower by phone, eagerly asking for information about the aircraft in flight.

"The flight continues as normal" said the colonel to his colleague after each information received.

"Fine" was just replying Wayne.

" Within a few minutes you will have arrived on the island taking the pictures. Within an hour, therefore, we will know what to expect about him.

"For you, more than anything, I want the eldest to come back showing us his innocence.

The minutes seemed to turn into centuries in that anguished wait. Colonel Burton did nothing to hide his nervousness. He had gotten up and was pacing up and down the room, taking long strides and making quick turns each time he came to the edge of the room. The slightly inclined sun entered through the windows, flooding the room with light, where the smoke from the cigarettes formed a thick cloud. The increasingly full ashtrays showed the prevailing nervousness. The two men at irregular intervals consulted their respective watches.

"We'll have news soon," Burton exclaimed.

"Yes, actually, there is little left for the precise time to have elapsed.

Sitting back down the colonel said:

"Despite having faith in the senior, I can't deny that I'm nervous.

"It is natural, the test is to define and for that reason his nervousness is understood.

Lighting a new cigarette, Colonel Burton asked with a certain sarcasm:

"If the elder returns, who will his suspicions fall on?

The question asked of Major Wayne left him somewhat surprised, but reacting, he replied:

"Particularly no one. I'm a bit puzzled, I confess, but in general about all the pilots and ground crew.

"It will be necessary to make a selection.

"Of course.

"Who will be the eldest among?

" Of course if he comes back, he will be in the 'non-suspect' selection.

"Well, now you can put him in the lead.

" He hasn't come back yet.

"But it won't be long before we hear of his return.

"Well then, but for now...

Burton interrupted the head of security by asking:

"So, all in all, you don't have any other suspects?

"Nope.

"And what do you plan to do? If the Italians continue to show us with their actions, that they know the day and time that we are going to attack them.

Wayne was silent as if considering the answer, although Burton knew for a fact that the military man did not know what to answer. The colonel with a certain irony asked:

"You'll keep looking, right ?

"Of course.

"That is his mission, but it is not only reduced to searching, he also has to find.

Major Wayne began to feel annoyed by his superior's words, and decided to bear his irony with resignation. The minutes passed slowly and it had been approximately fourteen since there had been any news of the major. Burton's nervousness increased.

"In a few minutes I should be here, right? Wayne asked.

"Yes.

"And there is no news of his return for now, it is something strange.

"A delay can be caused by anything.

"It's also true, but why don't you communicate it?

"He will know.

The hands of the clock continued indifferently, marking minute after minute, the time that passed.

CHAPTER XIII

THE FLIGHT

When Cameron took off from the Tobruk field, he realized that the mission he had been given was difficult to accomplish. The fact of having to photograph the enemy bases in full sun without an escort of any kind, was too exposed. The chances of success were extremely limited. However , the given order had to be carried out. The device flew in excellent conditions and the engine responded perfectly to the needs of the flight. In the cockpit of the Hurricane, the Major thought that he might not return to base. For a few moments he was completely sure of it. With great force of will, he pushed aside the macabre ideas that assailed him. He was a good pilot and had nothing to fear. The indicator devices on the dashboard made the major aware of the situation and the technical conditions in which he was making the crossing. At 8,000 feet the plane entered a strong updraft, which made it gain speed. Beneath the plane stretched out the blue sheet of the sea, in perfect calm, on which absolutely nothing stood out. The plane's propellers whistled as they cut off the supporting air and the plane was moving through it at high speed.

Pantelleria was still well to the north when Cameron saw an Italian plane fly over it about five hundred meters away. Apparently the Italian pilot had not noticed the presence of the British plane, so, ignoring it, he continued the flight above. Cameron for a few moments hesitated to attack him. It was possible that the Italian had actually seen him, but did not dare to attack him. In that case he would have communicated with the Pantelleria base and they would come out to meet him. Perhaps she hadn't seen him? Cameron decided not to rush him. The Italian apparatus was moving away, since the largest cut gas losing speed on purpose. The silhouette of the Italian plane was silhouetted in the distance, Cameron gained altitude and corrected the flight, since the wind that had risen from the east had caused him to enter a very pronounced angle of drift.

Pantelleria appeared in the distance, like a great cetacean floating in the waters. Boldly without thinking, for that was impossible, Cameron directed his craft toward the island in a straight line, without making a high-altitude tentative flight. It was getting closer to the island, which was increasing in size as the distance decreased. The contours of the island appeared clean. So far there had been no sign of aggression. After reviewing the cameras, Cameron prepared to launch himself on the island. Flying over the base, marked by Colonel Burton as being of prime interest, Cameron dove into it. When he got to the height he thought was safe, he pressed the automatic triggers of the cameras, and then took flight, satisfied with that first pass. In a circle, the major headed for the place where the coastal defenses were located. As he headed toward them, the island's anti-aircraft guns began firing at him. The clouds of explosions from the anti-aircraft shells surrounded the British plane, not yet hitting the target. With surprise, the major found that the Italians did not launch their aircraft on him, but limited themselves to fire from the ground, which was naturally to the major's liking. To avoid as much as possible the effectiveness of the defense pieces, Cameron lowered himself almost to the ground, thereby disconcerting the gunners of the pieces. On the military wharf, Cameron showed off his mastery as a pilot taking pictures over the wharfs at close range. He then gained height again and headed for the bases in the interior of the island. The fire from the defenses intensified somewhat as he entered. The pieces located in the mountains fired at him incessantly. After about four minutes of flight, he reached his destination where, outwitting the artillery with great danger, he carried out the operation with great skill.

The difficult part was already done. He was about to return to Tobruk, after taking the last photographs, stepping on the rudder, correcting flight, when suddenly, like true ghosts, five Italian hunting aircraft appeared in Cameron's sight. The eldest understood that his only salvation was to gain space for them, but the enemy aircraft were approaching at great speed, reaching him. The fight was going to be very unequal. By number the victory certainly belonged to the Italians. In a skillful and surprising maneuver, the largest dived passing under its enemies and placing itself behind their backs. Before they knew it, Cameron was charging at them, clanging his machine guns. The first bursts failed to hit the target, the projectiles being lost in the air, then falling on the ground of Pantelleria. The Italians, annoyed by the mockery of the British apparatus, threw themselves at Cameron almost at the same time. This let himself slip on the left wing, thus leaving the circle of fire formed by the machine guns of the five aircraft. After full throttle it rose at a steep angle, slamming into the tail of an enemy fighter. The major pressed the triggers of the machine guns and they began their stuttering song. The shells hit the target. The tail of the enemy aircraft was materially destroyed. Without flight control, the Italian plane went into a spin and crashed minutes later.

The remaining four aircraft, stung with self-esteem by the skill of that solitary man who so valiantly presented them with a face, threw themselves with desperate abandon at the Hurricane. The ground pieces had stopped firing, leaving the four aircraft to shoot down the enemy. Fatigue gave up the older Cameron, who heroically fought against his four enemies. Keeping the Italian planes at bay was a very difficult mission. However , the great skill and experience of the Englishman managed to make enemy planes fear to approach him.

Anguish crowded the older man's mind. His composure and skill made it clear to him that he was inevitably lost. The devices besieged him to the point of desperation. No matter how much effort the elder made, he couldn't get rid of them. The somewhat more skillful Hurricane in movement was the only advantage the elder had over his enemies. However , the numerical superiority was a very marked advantage over the largest, and this advantage was revealed.

The waters of the sea patiently lapped the shores of the island. The sky was calm again, while on the undulating surface of the water floated the remains of an airplane. On a piece of the fuselage, the marking of British aviation could be clearly distinguished. The twilight lights bathed the spaces, dyeing everything in bright colors. Silence fell, only perceiving the murmur produced by the waters in the continuous and monotonous breaking on the coast. Noise always the same, but always different. Little by little, the hundreds of stars miraculously suspended in it began to flicker in the infinity of the celestial vault, as a demonstration of the insignificance of the existence of man. Now the wise nature imposed as final mourning, the silence of the sidereal and the beauty of the incomprehensible. The roars of the cannons had ended as if ashamed of themselves, and the steel birds had suspended their artificial flight as if fearing to unleash the Creator's fury. The false succumbed under the effects of the natural, evil or struggle had not been able to destroy the beauty of the sunset, where the day dies or the night is born with its resounding silence, populated by mystery and beauty. Gleaming up there, the lights of the spaces judged the men, who perhaps with despotic malice looked enviously at what they would never understand. Where minutes before there had been a fight to the death between men, now peace reigned, and at the bottom of the waters of the seas were the residual evidence of what man calls "the art of war."

CHAPTER XIV

SENTENCE

The office clock said seven in the evening. Its tick-tock with undaunted march marked the time that was passing. Colonel Burton, his face drenched in sweat and visibly pale, drummed his fingertips on the desk in his office. In front of him was the head of the Security Service, who silently looked at his superior.

"Given the evidence of the facts, I must surrender," commented the colonel.

"My suspicions were not unfounded. The Major has not returned: He has stayed in Pantelleria with his family.

"It is possible that it was shot down.

"He would have notified us by radio that he was in combat.

"Who knows!

The two soldiers remained silent for a long time, each one sunk in their thoughts and ideas. Colonel Burton was really taken aback. It was impossible for him that the Major had anything to do with the enemy forces. Even checking the fact that Cameron did not return from his mission, it was hard to believe that he had stayed with the Italians. Shortly before eight o'clock at night, the head of auxiliary services notified the complete inefficiency of the radio search, because no matter how hard they did, they could not communicate with the compatriot plane.

"You win the game for the moment.

The Head of Security with satisfaction answered:

"I'm sorry for you.

"What difference does it make. Reality always prevails.

"That's true.

" And on this occasion the reality has been crushing for others, I had full confidence in the Major.

"You can never openly trust anyone. Experience proves it.

"This time, yes.

"What are you going to do? "asked the Head of Security.

"I nothing. You will attend and do the necessary paperwork to put an end to this matter.

"Yes sir.

"But...

"But what, sir? "asked the elder.

"What if they had shot it down?

"If so, we will find out.

"Well, let three days pass before doing anything.

"As you order.

"Yes, it is better. Let's leave a margin of time. We don't want to run too much and let's go catch our fingers.

The Security Chief smiled wryly as he said:

"You command.

Burton, buttoning up his tunic, made to leave the office, so the head of security stepped aside to give his superior a free pass.

"Thank you.

The colonel, almost without turning to look at the major, said goodbye to him saying:

"See you tomorrow. Goodnight.

The Head of Security gave his superior a military salute, but he was already walking away with a quick and determined step.

Burton couldn't sleep all night. Ideas and nightmares followed one another with incredible continuity. Two or three times he woke up in the middle of the night with a start, sweating and panting, feeling that something was wrong with him. Shrimp... Cameron... Inside the colonel something told him that the major was not a traitor, far from it. He had almost complete certainty that something bad had happened to him and that was why he had not come back. Burton had seen the Major fight on several occasions on different fronts and lines of fire. And always on all occasions he had behaved like a patriot and warrior. It was therefore quite impossible from Burton's point of view that the Major had turned out to be an Italian informer. The colonel wished for dawn. Perhaps with the light of the new day his worries would dissipate.

The control tower of the airfield was located in the right angle of it. It towered over the other base units, with a certain pride. The gallery that was at the top of it, completely made of glass, housed a long series of scientific devices, very useful for men in flight. From the simple anemometer to the radio beacon, there were all the necessary devices that every good command tower should have. Colonel Burton standing next to the transmitting apparatus, watching the same server that at equal intervals launched the call from the base into space. No matter how many times he called, no answer of any kind was obtained. The "listening" devices continually scanned the space for some sound that would soothe the base chief's mood. But it was all useless, completely useless. Major Cameron did not return.

"Anyway, keep watching and calling," the colonel ordered before leaving the tower.

"Yes, sir," replied the head of auxiliary services.

"Anything that happens let us know. It is of great interest to me.

"We will do it.

When Burton left the tower he felt an enormous weight on his soul. The disappointment he'd had seemed to have aged him a lot of years. With a slow step he went to his office, passing before by the base bar to have something to eat. When he entered said site he could realize that several pilots were talking about Major Cameron, and that when they saw him they stopped commenting. The officers respectfully saluted the colonel. In a corner of the room Lieutenants Leith and Powell entered, who, observing the state of the colonel, commented.

"From what you can see, it has affected him a lot that Major Cameron did not return.

"To some extent it is natural, Leith. I believe they have known each other for several years, and have repeatedly fought together.

"Then it is understood, but what about you, what do you think, what happened to the eldest? Tell me.

"Well, the most logical; they will have knocked it down. He left alone, I believe to fulfill a delicate mission. The Italians will have jumped on him.

"Pity.

"Yes, he was a good driver and a great teammate, although somewhat withdrawn.

"We all have our things.

"Certain.

The two officers continued to make comments. About fifteen minutes after the colonel entered the bar, a soldier with a hurried step approached him, and whispered a few words to him. Leaving lunch, he quickly left the room.

When the colonel arrived at the control tower, the lieutenant in charge of transmissions, after saluting, said:

"A submarine told us that yesterday at seven o'clock in the evening, when it was surfacing to recharge batteries, south of Pantelleria, it was able to clearly hear the noise of a battle in the direction of the island.

Burton remained silent with a slightly satisfied smile on his face. Then he asked:

"Nothing more?

"Yes, it informs us that due to the explosions, they have deduced that the fire was from pieces of earth.

" Anti-aircraft?

"Possibly, sir.

"Thank you.

Burton already knew that Cameron had defended himself bravely.

CHAPTER XV

IN ENEMY LANDS

Hands clenched on the rocks. With his body up to his chest in water, he was making real efforts to stay afloat. The slippery rocks due to the effect of the waters did not offer great security. The waves hit his back crushing his body against the rocks. Little by little and making great efforts, he rose, lifting his body out of the water. The wound on his thigh ached sharply and the blood he had lost had severely weakened him. At last, after long suffering, Cameron lay down on a flat rock. Through half-closed eyes he could see in the blackness of the night the twinkling of the stars. His uneven breathing revealed his weariness and exhaustion. The night protected him and his enemies, seeing that his plane plunged into the sea, had given him up for dead. Miraculously, however, the Major had managed to get out of the cockpit before the plane sank. Swimming was slowly approaching the shore. He remained lying on the rock for about half an hour, during which time his breathing evened out. It was six hours before dawn. Cameron thought that if the sun rose without him having a place to take refuge, he would be hopelessly a dead man. Making an effort , he sat up observing the place where he was. Suddenly in his imagination the images of a past were formed, he remembered that place, and he felt that in the midst of his tragedy a light of hope was opening.

The danger of being located by some Italian patrol existed in an overwhelming way. Crawling, jumping from cover to cover, Cameron made his way into the lands of Pantelleria. If his memory did not deceive him, he was near a village, where he had once had good friends. He also remembered that about three hundred meters from it there was a large mansion. Protected by darkness it was not very difficult to reach the town. Cameron discarded the idea of following rural roads, so his advance was made cross country, thus avoiding a large number of dangers. His injured leg faltered from time to time, falling twice to the ground, getting up again after long efforts. The terrain through which he was advancing was rocky and very uneven, so it offered great difficulties. Once he thought he heard voices a short distance from him, so he stood completely still listening. However, no matter how hard he tried, he heard nothing again. He thought that perhaps it was the result of his nervousness. The trunks of the trees that he began to find were a source of joy for him, since they offered him camouflage. Suddenly he felt his heart stop. He could clearly hear the engine of a car that, as its volume increased, indicated that it was approaching where he was. With great caution he lay down on the ground and waited. He felt his heart pounding and his hands were drenched in cold sweat. The blackness of those places was broken by the headlights of a car that, taking a curve, passed close to him. His hands were nailed to the ground in a rictus of anguish and despair. The car drove away, darkness and silence spreading again. Getting up again, he began the march, through the insecure terrain. The trees, like ghosts, rose from the ground imposing their mass. Cameron felt weak at times and came to doubt if he would reach the destination point that had been proposed. He knew positively that to the place where he was going he could count on safe and noble friends. After two hours of walking, through those places that years before he had traveled in the most absolute calm, he reached a promontory . On the ground below him, several lights could be seen flickering faintly, indicating the existence of buildings. Studying the position of those lights, Cameron made sure where he was with great precision. Determined, he started walking. Suddenly he felt his feet get damp. He stopped and, bending down, verified with joy that a small stream ran at his feet. Making a saucepan with his hands, the Major drank the rich and fresh water, with which he felt comforted. After drinking, he thought that he had plenty of time to get to the village, and then he decided to rest a bit. Sitting on a thick rock, he remained motionless as he felt his heart pounding. The images of the past piled up in his mind, struggling against each other to remain retained, but the succession of ideas, born in the memories, pushed the images in a rapid and tumultuous parade.

Perhaps he had slept. When the Major raised his head from the palms of his hands, the stars were still shining in space and the lights of the houses twinkled in the town. More relieved after the break, he decided to continue walking. His legs responded somewhat better to the needs of the march, although the thigh wound ached intensely. Although he could walk faster, he did it slowly and with more precautions. Being closer to the small village meant refuge on the one hand and increased danger on the other. The descent down the slope, toward the town, was a promise of safety and danger, a congruence that tormented the Major. The night was still completely closed and behind Cameron's back, black mists began to rise on the horizon, which tended to increase its darkness. His hands were bleeding. His groping made him lose his balance, so several times his hands clung to bushes and sharp plants that hurt him. The insecurity of the march was exhausting, due to the irregularity of the terrain, which on several occasions suddenly changed its configuration. Twice he seemed to hear the Major voices not far from him. Both times he held his breath, wanting not to cause the slightest noise. The first time he could not be sure if they were really talking, but the second time, with great horror he could hear voices approaching him. Apparently they were two men. They spoke Italian correctly and Cameron was able to hear part of a conversation.

"Brave jerk. Look to come alone.

"It's not important. Now he is out of action.

"He gave a lot to do... "It 's true but in the end...

"The water.

"Yes...

The conversation was quite clear, so that the Major did not understand that those men were talking about him. Straining his ears, he heard:

"Tomorrow they will dredge the place where it has fallen, since it has ended up on the sandbanks. So we'll see what face it has.

"Yes.

"And also how riddled he will be. They will have put a good ration of lead.

"Sure.

The two men laughed boisterously. By the time they stopped doing so and resumed their conversation, they had already moved considerably away, so that the major could only catch a couple of words on the fly.

"The lieutenant...says...

What would happen when they discovered that he was not inside the device? This was the immediate question that the Major asked himself, answering himself quickly:

"They will not leave a stone unturned until they find me.

"The situation was difficult, more than he had believed. The events had increased the major's nervous tension. With horror he saw that the lights of the town danced before his eyes. He felt his legs trembling, and clinging tightly to a branch, he held on for a few moments and then slipped. His knees touched the ground, everything clouded before his eyes and, fainted, he fell prone on the ground. The thigh wound was bleeding profusely.

CHAPTER XVI

THE ENCOUNTER

When Cameron opened his eyes he thought he was dreaming, because before him he saw the beautiful and youthful face of a girl who leaned over his face looking at him with some admiration. As in these cases, Cameron asked:

"Where I am?

The young woman smiled at him and with a sweet and consoling accent answered the anxious question:

"It is in a quiet place, I can assure you.

Cameron smiled and closing his eyes remained silent as he listened to his companion's measured breathing. For a few moments he thought he smelled a faint, pleasant feminine scent, and he felt his heart speed up. After keeping his eyes closed for a few minutes, he opened them again and saw that the young girl was gone. Unhurriedly, he looked around the room where he was. It was a large room, with a brick-red floor and snow-white walls, from which hung a few pictures with a variety of motifs. In a corner he could see an old dark wood cabinet with a large mirror, in it he could see the reflection of the window that was almost at the head of his bed. He was so engrossed in his observations that he did not notice that the young woman who had previously been with him was re-entering the room carrying civilian clothes on her arms. The young woman approaching the bed asked:

"How are you?

Turning to her, Cameron replied:

"Fairly recovered.

" It's natural. He has slept almost eight hours and we have treated the wound he has on his muscle.

"Thank you very much.

As if guessing the series of questions that were piling up in Cameron's mind, the young woman said:

"My brother found him lying on the ground and very carefully brought him home. My father is a doctor and he says that what you have is nothing serious, you.

A visibly pleased Cameron replied.

"I'm in good hands by the looks of it.

The young woman, looking up and fixing her eyes on Cameron's, commented with a certain arrogance:

"You can be sure of it.

I didn't mean to offend her with my comment.

"Of course I know.

The young woman had left the clothes on Cameron's bed and, giving him a smile, said:

"Get up, dress in civilian clothes and go downstairs. My father wants to talk to him.

"Good.

"If you need anything call.

"Thank you.

With a quick step the young woman headed for the door, leaving the room.

While the eldest dressed in those clothes, consisting of corduroy pants and a flannel shirt, as well as some old hiking boots, he wondered, calming his nerves and promising himself good luck.

The stairs by which he went down to the ground floor were wooden and quite worn. When he reached the last steps of it, he could see before him, a large and magnificent room, in the center of which was a large table. He was looking at everything that appeared before his eyes, when he heard a manly voice that calmly told him:

"Come on, Major, sit down.

Cameron turned to where the voice had come from. He made out an elderly man with a trimmed beard, who was directing him to a seat. The young man obeyed and the other explained, anticipating his words:

"When my son Olaf brought you you were unconscious, but I could immediately see that you would recover quickly. He paused and then added: My name is Nissen and I am a doctor. We have lived here with my children for many years. As we are Swedish subjects, we belong to a neutral nation and the Italians have not bothered us. And by the way, these will be looking for you now. They have realized that he did not die and must remain hidden at home.

"I appreciate it, but I expose them to enormous risk.

Nissen shrugged.

"Life is a series of risks. You yourself have taken a great risk.

Cameron nodded.

"I was miraculously saved.

"You can tell.

" I still don't understand how I got out alive from the attacks of the Italian fighters.

"It just wasn't his time. When this one arrives there will be no human force capable of saving him.

"Is right.

"Now come on. You need to get your strength back and that can only be achieved with a good lunch.

"Again you are right.

Rising, they went to the table in the room where the young woman who had originally attended the elder had served a hearty lunch.

"My daughter has a great hand in the kitchen.

"So it seems" replied Cameron looking at the food.

"Sit down and eat as much as you like.

"Thank you.

Obeying, Cameron began to eat with great appetite. During lunch little was said. Toward the end of it, a stout-looking young man suddenly entered the dining room panting, and in a voice cracking with fatigue he said:

"They are searching the town, house by house! It won't take long for the patrol to get here!

They all fell silent looking at each other. Suddenly the old man stood up and said:

"You must hide. Go with him, Olaf; you know where The old man gestured for the elder to follow the young man.

Cameron asked:

"My uniform?

"Do not be afraid. It's turned into a pile of ashes.

"That's fine.

In an impatient and uneasy voice, Olaf exclaimed:

"Come on, hurry up!

Cameron followed the young man, starting up the stairs. Suddenly they reached Cameron, a loud knocking on the front door.

"They are already here! Olaf exclaimed.

"Yes, they must be.

"Come on, come on quickly!

When they reached a second floor, they walked down a long corridor to a room. Once inside, Olaf walked over to a chest of drawers, and pulling it back from the wall revealed a small door.

"Enter without fear. It will be safe. Don't worry. When they are gone we will let you know.

Somewhat nervous Cameron did as he was told.

CHAPTER XVII

A DISCOVERY

Dimly, the voices of the soldiers searching the house reached Cameron. With his nerves in tension, he remained motionless, awaiting events. Suddenly he became aware that the voices were increasing in volume. Italian soldiers were in the room, which led to their hiding place. Her heart was beating fast and she could clearly hear their conversation.

"We are certain, doctor, that the Englishman we shot down is alive and hiding on the island.

"I understand, but looking for him should not be an easy task.

"Yourself...

Cameron was amazed at the tranquility shown by his friend the doctor.

"Don't you have any clues?

"This is the town that is closest to the point where your device fell, so we have started the search here. I beg your pardon for the inconvenience.

"There was no more. You fulfill your obligation.

"Of course.

"You don't have to apologize.

"Thank you, we see that there is no one here. If you allow us, we will continue.

"Yes, yes, continue.

With joy, Cameron realized that the enemy soldiers were moving away. Little by little, while he was waiting for them to come and take him out of his hiding place, he became aware of the darkness of the place where he was. When his eyes became accustomed to the weak and dim light, he saw before him some disorderly furniture. On a table placed in a corner of the tiny room where he was, he saw a pile of papers. With almost mechanical movements he began to leaf through said papers, some of which fell to the ground. Cameron bent down to pick them up, and great was his surprise when he found a photograph, of a person he knew. As his eyes fastened on the image depicted on the small paper quadrangle, he felt a terrible emotion. He remained absolutely still for a few moments and then with a nervous gesture he put the photo in his pants pocket. After an indeterminate amount of time for the eldest, he felt this noise again in the room, which gave way to his hiding place. Suddenly he heard a voice asking.

"Are you okay, Major?

Cameron recognized Michael's voice and answered.

"Yes.

"Now I will bring him out of hiding. The danger has passed.

"Fine thanks.

When the eldest found himself back on the ground floor of the building, in the company of his new friends, he asked:

"What happened?

The old man with a friendly expression, approaching the elder and taking him by the arm, said:

"Nothing, nothing in particular.

"They look for me?

"Yes, that is.

"Maybe they'll come back?

"Could be, but not for now.

"Good.

The old doctor sat down in a chair and after resting for a few minutes said:

"My daughter says that the Italians are absolutely certain that you are in this town. We thought it would be convenient for you to get out of it.

" But how?

With his right hand the old man scratched his beard and after meditating for a few moments he exclaimed.

"Is not difficult.

"Expose.

"You see, we know of some secret passageways that lead to the seashore. They are ancient water currents that over time have lost their liquid element and have left behind a series of secret tunnels...

"And what would he gain by reaching the sea?

"My son Michael would provide him with a rubber boat and food. With this you can get closer to the areas frequented by compatriot boats.

Cameron seemed to consider the words of his rescuer, after a few moments in which he remained silent, during which he did not take his eyes off the doctor's daughter, whose name was Signe. At last he said:

"It's risky, but I think it's my only chance.

"Yes it is.

"Okay, so when?

"Morning.

"In agreement.

During that night Cameron could not sleep, his thoughts flew to what lay ahead. Launching into the open sea in a rubber boat, and surrounded by enemies, was not an easy task. However , he understood that it was his salvation, because the Italians would leave no stone unturned until they found him. He was in great danger staying in that house, and besides, for its owners it was a great commitment. Decidedly, it was his duty. During the night he was assailed by the most terrible nightmares. He thought he was always surprised by the Italians and on other occasions he thought he saw the young Signe, martyred by the enemies, subjected to harsh interrogations. However , the light of dawn dissipated their sufferings.

When he went down to the dining room, everyone was waiting for him. Cameron felt annoyed at such kindness, for he had never been able to think of such help.

"Hello. How have you slept?

Lying Cameron replied:

"Good very good.

"We are glad about it.

After lunch, during which a close watch was kept in case the Italians approached the house, Cameron, taking from his pants pocket the photograph he had found, in the place that served as a hiding place, asked:

"Do you know this individual?

The photograph passed from hand to hand and everyone denied knowing him.

"However: I was at your house though!

The old doctor replied:

"We do not doubt it, because I myself have seen this photograph on another occasion.

"How?

"You see, in this house about a year ago, the Italian high command was, and a series of meetings or conferences were held in it. That photograph that you found during your confinement in the room was forgotten by one of those who were here. Understands?

"You mean it belongs to an Italian?

"Yes, to a chief of the Italian General Staff.

Cameron was silent for a few moments, and then in a slow and complacent voice he said:

"Thanks for the clarification.

"They don't deserve, and speaking of something else. Are you ready to leave tonight?

"Yes.

"Well, my son Olaf will give you all sorts of details.

"It's okay.

Cameron looked askance at Signe who was sitting next to him and noticed the great emotion that seized her.

CHAPTER XVIII

RETURN

"Good luck to you, Major.

"Thank you, Olaf. I will never forget your help.

"It's not important.

"Yes it does. More than you imagine.

The night was completely closed. The sky covered with black clouds stole all visibility. The waters of the sea were serene. They had already placed all the provisions in the rubber boat. Cameron held out his hand to Olaf as he said:

Goodbye and good luck, I'll be back.

"Until another.

The raft floated on the waters with great agility, little by little it was moving away from the coast, and therefore entering the waters. The small compass that Olaf had given to the eldest was enough for him to orient himself in the middle of the liquid element. Not the slightest light was seen and blackness was the owner of the space. The spirit of Major Cameron, was overwhelmed by the horror of that night, gave the feeling of being in a non-existent world.

The Major had already been sailing for three hours when he decided to check the route he was following. Using the chart and compass, provided by Olaf, Cameron made sure he was heading in the right direction. The events that hours before had lived, remained alive in the Major's mind. He seemed to hear Signe's faint voice waving him off, as well as her eyes full of tears that she wanted to hide behind a delicious shame.

The sea breeze whispered in the Major's ears, the water remained calm and the temperature was pleasant. At eight forty in the morning, Cameron estimated that he had covered a little less than half the distance that separated him from his compatriots. The breeze that had been blowing all night, billowed the small sails of his boat, pushing him towards his destination. The lights of dawn illuminated the surface of the sea that appeared clean and serene, except for the natural undulations. At ten o'clock, they passed about fifty meters away from where Cameron was, a flock of dolphins, jumping out of the water, exposing their metallic backs. The show was beautiful. The speed reached by these fish was extraordinary, and in a few minutes they had disappeared, the sight. About eleven o'clock the oldest could hear the engine of an aircraft. He looked for it in the blue of the sky, and at last he distinguished it far to the north and quite high. He remained for a few seconds with his eyes fixed on the device, until he was sure that it was Italian. Perhaps they were looking for him? Camarón understood how difficult it was to locate him, since he was nothing more than an invisible point in an immense plain.

Four hours had passed since Cameron saw the Italian aircraft, when in front of him, to the south, he could make out the plume of smoke, left by a ship. Uneasiness washed over him. The safest thing was that that ship was English, because it sailed very far south, and until now the enemy squadron had not dared to go so far. With his binoculars he looked anxiously towards the place from which the column of thick black smoke was issuing. But a light fog prevented the older man from clearly distinguishing the characteristics of the ship.

Within an hour, Cameron was able to ascertain that the ship was British, and that the route it was following was approaching him. The joy overwhelmed him and with his nerves in tension, he waited for the moment in which he was saved. The wind had increased in volume, as had the waves, so the little boat danced on the water. Each time he sank into the belly formed between wave and wave, the ship disappeared from his sight, but when it was raised again by a body of water, the silhouette of the ship appeared before him again.

Standing on top of the boat, swinging his shirt on the end of his oar, Major Cameron was trying to get the attention of the ship's crew, which was a relatively short distance from him. In its navigation, the ship had described a semicircle for what had been traced on its route. Cameron screamed with all his might. Suddenly, to the infinite joy of the major, the ship made a discharge, with one of its bow pieces. They had seen him!

When Cameron finished eating, he leaned back in his comfortable seat and for a few moments was silent, watching the first officer of the ship that had picked him up. The officer, a distinguished-looking young man, leaned over Cameron with a smiling expression, asking:

"Replacement?

Cameron in a slow and unhurried voice, after taking a long, deep breath, replied:

"Something.

The cabin was small but comfortable , with all the comforts that could be asked for and desired on board a warship. Through the small peephole that led to the outside, the sun entered happily, while the ship at full speed headed for the coast of North Africa.

"In an hour we will be on the ground.

"How glad I am.

"Of course, major" said the ship's officer with a complacent voice, "your odyssey is worth telling, among the great episodes.

Cameron making a negative gesture with his head, commented:

" Don't believe it, what has happened to me is very common among aviators. And by the way, have you notified Tobruk Air Base of my encounter?

"Yes, your bosses already know that you have been picked up by us.

"I'm glad, they'll be calmer that way.

"Of course, we have received a note from your colonel, expressing his delight to hear that you are safe and sound, and that you are returning to base.

On deck, Cameron watched the shore as they incessantly approached. The powerful machines of the ship, pushed with vigorous impulse to the enormous mass of steel towards its destination. With emotion and almost incredulity, the eldest contemplated the land that for him was a promise.

"We're here" commented the first officer approaching the major.

"Yes, and I really feel excited.

"I understand.

The ship approached the mooring docks and after skillful maneuvering, it was stuck to the cement banks. Looking back, Cameron looked at the great plain of water with a certain irony. Then he turned to the officer and said:

"Well, I have already arrived. I thank you for what you have done for me.

"It was my obligation as a compatriot.

"However, I thank you.

The first officer shaking hands with Cameron said:

"Good luck, friend.

"Thank you and likewise.

"It is to be expected.

Somewhat nervously, Cameron jumped ship. When he was on the firm ground of the dock, he turned to him and waved his hand at the officer who returned the salute from the deck. Cameron mumbled:

"«Blessed be you, friend...»

Minutes later the British ship resumed its march, after having returned a compatriot to the mainland.

CHAPTER XIX

A POINT IS CLARIFIED

Colonel Burton's joy at learning of Major Cameron's return knew no bounds. The head of security seemed to be happy, but deep down the major's return represented a failure for him, and it hurt him. Burton, his face glowing with emotion, was talking his head off, in abundant verbiage.

"I have won the game, Cameron is back!

"I know," replied the older Wayne.

"Your prophecies have been wrong, because in a few minutes you will be here. It will surely bring interesting information for us, not for the Italians.

Burton's words struck at the major, who patiently listened to his superior's speech, not daring to reply.

During the waiting time until the arrival of the elder, his comrades prepared a reception for his arrival. Shortly after noon, the roar of a car engine was heard, and the shouting of some pilots.

"It's here! exclaimed the colonel, standing up suddenly.

Indeed, a " jeep " was coming across the field, in which the eldest was riding. His companions ran to meet Cameron, who answered their greetings with great joy.

When, minutes later, Major Cameron was in Colonel Burton's office, the latter asked him to tell him in detail what had happened to him. At the end of his explanation Cameron turning to the head of security said:

"For you I bring a data of great interest.

"Which?

Playing the lazy, Cameron smiling said:

"I am in a position to tell you with complete certainty who is the individual who makes the defenders of Pantelleria aware of our interventions.

Surprise and curiosity mirrored Wayne's face. Without being able to avoid it, he asked:

"Who?

The major seemed ready to torment Wayne, as he was in no hurry to clear things up. Burton on the other hand showed no great interest in the matter. Finally, after taking great detours, Cameron took the photograph found in the house of his rescuers out of his jacket pocket and handed it over to Colonel Burton, who, having it in his hands and seeing it, exclaimed:

" Gardener !

Rising from his seat, the major moved to Burton's side and fixed his gaze on the photograph.

"It's possible?

The eldest, undeterred, explained how he had found that photograph.

"So it is Captain Tom Gardiner , the Italian informer?

"There is no doubt, sir, in the photograph that I have given you, the captain appears in an Italian uniform. It is therefore he who informs.

Burton turning to the security chief said:

"Stop him immediately and bring him to me.

"Yes sir.

Obeying Wayne's order, he left the office, leaving the older man with the colonel, who continued talking when the head of security left, but in a less official tone and more like colleagues. Half an hour later, the head of security entered again, accompanied by Captain Gardiner , who greeted the major effusively. Colonel Burton, calmly after the first few moments, asked:

" Could you do me a favor, Captain?

Gardiner with great fervor answered:

"Of course, sir.

"Well, then, you want to explain to us what this photograph means.

Burton handed the captain his photograph. The officer seemed to freeze, his face took on the expressionlessness of granite, and in the most impressive of silences he looked at the photograph. The head of security said:

"I'm sorry, captain, but my obligation is to stop you.

"I'm sorry too," Burton commented.

The captain put the photograph back on the table and, turning to the major, stared at him fixedly. Cameron, observing the captain's gaze, explained:

"It is a bad habit to leave behind forgotten photographs. I found it by chance.

The captain, giving a deep sigh and without losing the cold blood he had shown, said to the colonel:

"You have won.

"Yes, fortunately.

"I have done nothing more than comply with what my commanders ordered me to do.

"I know, you were doing your duty by informing your people, but it's over, they won't have any more confirmations of our attacks.

The head of security remained silent, awaiting the order to withdraw with the prisoner, to subject him to an intense interrogation. Burton, once the captain's guilt was confirmed, left him in the hands of the head of security.

"One less enemy" said the colonel to the major once they were alone.

"Yes it's correct.

"And think that...

"What?

" Nothing, it doesn't matter.

The three Channel Islands were subjected to intense bombardment and a total blockade, so the defense of the three islands began to weaken, even more so when the defense garrisons began to run out of supplies.

Major Cameron, flight after flight, became aware of the continued weakness of the island, so he understood that it would not take long to surrender. Twice in his flights, after completing his mission, he entered the terrain of the island, flying over the house of his rescuers, who immediately understood who was piloting that device.

Arms crossed over his chest, the colonel asked:

"What's up, Cameron?

"The Italians won't last long. In each flight that he made, he noticed a great loss, in the defensive fire.

"Maybe it will be a matter of two or three days.

"I think so.

"And then to Sicily.

Burton walked over to a map hanging on the wall and, fixing his eyes on the island of Sicily, said:

"With this, we will initiate the end of the war.

"God willing.

"And the men too. What do you plan to do when the war is over?

Cameron without the slightest hesitation replied:

"If I make it out alive, I will look for a good job with an airline company.

"And as for getting married?

"If there is an opportunity, why not?

The two soldiers will continue talking for a long time, about various topics, leaving aside the war and its complications.

The combat apparatuses landed and took off continuously from the Tobruk base, to continue crushing the terrain of the three islands, which , in plain sight, were losing defense capacity.

CHAPTER XX

DESTINY

The device was moving on what had been a vital point of defense for Pantelleria. Landing units of the English forces had touched the coast of the island, and the Italians gave themselves up, offering no resistance. The English recognized that the enemies had behaved heroically in the defense of that handful of land, but the lack of water, food and ammunition had accelerated the defeat of the Italians.

After the observation flight over the island, Cameron returned to the new Pantelleria base, once the auxiliary services teams had filled the funnels produced in the airfield by the bombs dropped in the continuous and heavy bombardment. Giving some humps, due to the faulty runway, the major landed, for the first time with his plane on the island. He directed his plane towards the group, and once in it, he removed contact, stopping the engine.

The sun beat down hard on the road. Through it the open car, in which Cameron was riding, ran at a brisk pace. After about half an hour of travel, they reached the top of a small rise in the ground, behind which appeared the village, in which the elder had found protection. From up there, he searched with some anxiety for the house in which he wanted to find himself. To the right, neat and proud, stood the two-story house. Cameron was excited as the car began to roll toward the building.

Olaf had gone out almost at a run to meet the elder, the doctor appeared behind him. Cameron warmly greeted the two but was nonetheless somewhat disheartened when he failed to see Signe. The old doctor, as if guessing the wishes of the elder, said:

" Women are flirty. Sometimes they spend half an hour fighting a ripple, which wanders from where it should be, but I don't think the battle will last long.

Cameron, relieved by the doctor's words, replied:

"Now I understand.

For about ten minutes, protected from the sun under a cane awning, the doctor explained to the elder how the Italians had been losing strength, until the moment of surrender arrived.

"Did they search them again?

"No, they didn't have time.

The three men continued talking until...

Signe was beautiful, very beautiful, and Cameron felt a shock as the young woman suddenly appeared before him, perhaps with studied movements and rehearsed expressions. The eldest stood up and holding out his hand to Signe, the only thing that occurred to him was to say:

"Hello.

The most determined young woman showed great joy at the elder's return, and besieged him with questions about his trip back to Africa, and other things.

Whistling happily, Cameron leaned against a can of gasoline as he watched his device being checked over. Suddenly someone asked him behind his back:

"What is this joy?

As the Major turned, he saw the Colonel looking at him with a frown. Cameron, forgetting military formalities, asked point blank:

"Could I go out to dinner tonight?

"A permit?

"Yes.

"We'll discuss it over a beer, okay?

" For me, yes.

"So let's go.

Burton showed great sympathy for Cameron. Putting his hand on the elder's shoulder, he said:

"Maybe it's the last beer we drink together...

"How?

"Tomorrow I am going back to Tobruk, and you will stay here until further orders. Who knows where they will go? And because this is the last time, perhaps, that he asks me for a permit, I give it to him.

"Thank you.

"And where do you intend to go?

In a few words, Cameron explained his meeting with those who had saved his life, and that he was also invited that night to have dinner with them. Burton smiling and tapping his nose with the tip of his index finger said:

"It smells like singe to me.

"To singe?

"Well, to the wedding.

"God will say.

Taking the last sip of beer, Burton said:

"God has already said it.

Burton walked away, while a smiling Cameron watched him.

The day was dying when Cameron sat in the back seat of the official car, headed for the Clift house, his imagination materialized Signe's face, and Limerón felt great desire to be with her.

Dr. Ruter Clift, while filling his guest's glass, observed that he did not take his eyes off his daughter and his quick understanding made him see what was going to happen.

"Do you like the island?

Cameron, as if coming out of a dream, replied:

"Yes. I already knew her, about fifteen years ago I was here.

"It is interesting...

But Cameron hardly paid attention to what they said. He saw nothing but Signe's beautiful face, and heard nothing but Colonel Burton's voice saying, "GOD HAS ALREADY SAID IT."

END

9 798231 621644